FOR MARILYN, WITH BREEZY LOVE —L.G.S.

FOR LISA —L.W.

Text copyright © 2018 by Liz Garton Scanlon
Jacket art and interior illustrations copyright © 2018 by Lee White

All rights reserved. Published in the United States by Schwartz & Wade Books,
an imprint of Random House Children's Books, a division of Penguin Random House LLC, New York.

Schwartz & Wade Books and the colophon are trademarks of Penguin Random House LLC.

Visit us on the Web! rhcbooks.com

Educators and librarians, for a variety of teaching tools, visit us at RHTeachersLibrarians.com

Library of Congress Cataloging-in-Publication Data
Names: Scanlon, Elizabeth Garton, author. | White, Lee, illustrator.
Title: Kate, who tamed the wind / by Liz Garton Scanlon ; illustrated by Lee White.
Description: First edition. | New York : Schwartz & Wade Books, an imprint of Random House Children's Books, [2018]
Summary: A young girl finds a way to tame the winds besieging an old man who lives on a hill above her village.
Identifiers: LCCN 2016057421 | ISBN 978-1-101-93479-1 (hc) | ISBN 978-1-101-93480-7 (glb) | ISBN 978-1-101-93481-4 (epub)
Subjects: | CYAC: Winds—Fiction. Classification: LCC PZ7.S2798 Kat 2018 | DDC [E]—dc23

The text of this book is set in 13.5-point Deccan.
The illustrations were rendered in mixed media (watercolor, ink, digital).

MANUFACTURED IN CHINA
2 4 6 8 10 9 7 5 3 1
First Edition

KATE, WHO TAMED THE WIND

words by LIZ GARTON SCANLON

illustrations by LEE WHITE

schwartz & wade books · new york

and blew....

and blew...

The wind blew until the shutters banged in the creaky house on the tip-top of the steep hill.

The wind blew, the shutters banged, and the boards bent.

The man lived all alone
in the creaky house on the
tip-top of a steep hill where
a soft wind blew.

The man lived all alone
in the creaky house where the
curtains swung and chimes spun
as a soft wind blew . . .

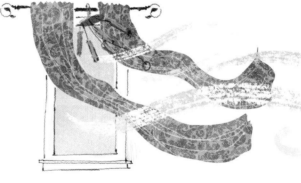

Once there was a man living all alone in a creaky house on the tip-top of a steep hill.

The wind blew, the shutters banged, the boards bent, the table tipped, and the tea spilled.

The tea spilled and the bread broke on the tippy table in the creaky house at the tip-top of the steep hill.

And still the wind blew.

The wind blew, and
off the birds flew.

The birds flew and
the dust did, too,
and the man cried,

What to do?

What to do?

The wind whipped his words from the
tip-top of the steep hill to the itty-bitty
town at the bottom, where a little girl
called Kate heard the cry—and felt it, too.

She wondered what
on earth to do!

?. wind?.

NEW
TREES

Kate could not stop the wind,
she knew, but . . .

CHALK

she could wheel a load of
new trees to the tip-top
of the dusty hill in her wagon.

There, Kate dug deep holes and watered muddy mounds . . .

till the trees grew.

As the trees grew, the wind blew.

The trees grew,
the wind blew,

and the time flew.

The time
flew as the
trees grew . . .

and grew . . .

. . . and Kate did, too.

The trees grew till the leaves
fluttered and the shutters stilled
and the boards bounced back.

The leaves fluttered, the shutters stilled, the
boards bounced back, and the dust died down.

The dust died down, the tea steeped,
and the birds peeped.

The birds peeped and the old man poured sweet tea and said, "For you!" near the quiet house on the tip-top of the green hill . . .

where a bright breeze blew.

MORE ABOUT MARVELOUS TREES

Trees are an important part of Earth's ecosystem—they play a starring role in keeping our planet beautiful, healthy, and productive. Most people know that trees provide shade on hot days, fruit for breakfast, and home to all sorts of birds and wildlife. They're good for swinging and climbing, too. But did you know trees also work invisibly while they're growing your peaches and holding your hammock?

Trees act like lungs—they clean the air by absorbing or "inhaling" carbon dioxide gas created by people, animals, and oceans and "exhaling" the oxygen we need to survive. They also work underground, filtering groundwater through their roots and preventing flooding and erosion by holding soil in place.

My favorite trees are aspens, with their silvery bark and their bright gold leaves in the fall. Aspens seem to know that by sticking together, they can make a difference—they live in great big colonies, or families, connected by their roots, and together they fill their mountainside homes with beauty, birdsong, and fresh air.

The little girl in this story made a difference with her wagon full of saplings, too. They served as a windbreak, they held the dust down, and they provided shade, homes for birds and squirrels, and happiness. Yep, she made a difference, and you can, too! Here's how:

- Paper is made from trees. Use less of it, don't be wasteful, and recycle.

- Learn about what trees need to stay healthy, and help where you can.

- Plant a tree in your own backyard, in a park nearby, or at the tip-top

  of a very steep hill!

Here are some marvelous folks supporting our marvelous planet by protecting marvelous forests and planting marvelous trees. Join them!

arborday.org

friendsoftrees.org

rainforest-alliance.org

treesforthefuture.org

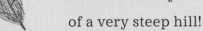